Ladybird

This Little Story

belongs to

_____

Published by Ladybird Books Ltd
27 Wrights Lane London W8 5TZ
A Penguin Company
5 7 9 10 8 6

© LADYBIRD BOOKS LTD MCMXCVII

Printed in Italy

Noisy
Little
Truck

by Nicola Baxter
illustrated by Harmen van Straaten

It was another beautiful day in the quiet little square.

Swish! Swoosh! The storekeeper swept the steps of her shop.

Snipper! Snip! The hairdresser busily whizzed with her scissors.

Splish! Splosh! High on a ladder, right at the top, a workman was painting the town hall clock.

There was not another sound to be heard.

But just then…

SNIPPER

Handy

there was a *rattle* and a *rumble* and a *jangle*, *screech*, *vroom*! And everything shivered and shook.

"It's an earthquake!" gasped the storekeeper, diving for cover.

"An avalanche!" squealed the hairdresser, clutching her curlers.

"A disaster!" cried the workman, dropping his paint pot. "Look out below!"

But it wasn't an earthquake, or an avalanche, or a disaster. It was…

just one little truck, travelling too fast and making *much* too much noise!

The Little Truck braked with a *squeal* and a *BEEP*!

"Important deliveries here for the store! I'll be driving in daily to bring you some more!"

"*Every* day?" asked the hairdresser, faintly.

"We do *need* deliveries every day," sighed the storekeeper.

"What we *need*," said the painter, "is some *warning*. Why not come at lunchtime, Little Truck, when I'm *not* up my ladder? And a little less speedy, if you please."

"No problem!" called the cheerful Little Truck.

Next morning, all was quiet in
the square.

The painter finished the town hall
clock and set it going again. *Tick! Tock!*

The storekeeper chopped and
wrapped and weighed.

The hairdresser cut and curled
and sprayed.

At lunchtime, old Mr McCrumb came
out to feed the birds. And everyone
else sat down in the sun.

But just as the hairdresser poured
out her soup...

the painter picked up
his sandwich...

and the storekeeper
settled down for
a snooze...

there was a *rattle* and a *rumble* and a *jangle*, *screech*, *BEEP*! The noisy Little Truck *did* try to drive with more care, but *still* everything shivered and shook.

The hairdresser's soup was spilled with a *gloop*!

The painter's sandwich dropped with a *plop*!

Oh no!

And the storekeeper fell off her chair.

Not again!

The Little Truck parked.
"Was that better?" he asked.

The storekeeper started, "Let me put it like this…"

"I've been shampooed with soup!" screeched the hairdresser, dripping.

"I've pilchards in my paint!" moaned the workman, fishing.

The Little Truck thought, "I've a brilliant idea! I'll come at a time when *no one* is here."

Next day, the square was quiet
and still.

No sandwiches jumped and no soup
was spilled.

But, when everyone was tucked up
in bed, at the very quietest time of
the night…

there was a *rattle* and a *rumble* and a *jangle*, *BEEP*! And though it was quieter than during the day, still *lots* of things shivered and shook.

Old Mr McCrumb tumbled *bump,* out of bed!

The painter's whole family woke up and said, "What was *that*?"

And the storekeeper opened her door with a *crash*!

"If that's you-know-who, it's not funny," she called. "I'm going to sort this out *once and for all*!"

So down in the square, in some *very* strange clothes, everyone gathered to grumble and groan.

"I'm sorry to say, all my pigeons have gone!" said old Mr McCrumb.

"*Something* must be done!" the hairdresser agreed.

"I *am* driving more slowly," said the noisy Little Truck, sadly. "I can't help *some* rumbling. I'm a *truck*, after all!"

It was hard to be cross with the poor Little Truck.

"It *can't* really be easy, with a big, heavy load," agreed Mr McCrumb.

Then the painter's small daughter had her own bright idea. She stood on her tiptoes to reach her dad's ear.

She whispered. He listened. The whisper went round. And so did a smile as big as the town!

For the rest of the night, not a sound could be heard, except for some snoring and the homecoming birds.

Then, just as the sun slipped into
the sky…

there was a *rattle* and a *rumble* and a *beep*, *beepity*, *BEEP*! At once the whole town was awake.

"Well *done*, Little Truck," they all came out to say.

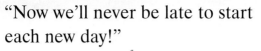

"Now we'll never be late to start
each new day!"